The Little Things

A Collection of Short Stories

Michael Wade

This book is a work of fiction. Names, characters, businesses, organizations, places, events, and incidents either are the product of the author's imagination or are used fictitiously. Any resemblance to actual persons, living or dead, events or locales is entirely coincidental.

CLF Publishing, LLC.
9161 Sierra Ave, Ste. 203C
Fontana, CA 92335
www.clfpublishing.org

Cover Design by Senir Design. Contact information-info@senirdesign.com.

ISBN #978-1-945102-14-1

Printed in the United States of America.

To my brothers: Justin and Austin

Table of Contents

Kendra

Nobody knows the real you. They only know you by whatever mask you are wearing at the moment. Those who know you from elementary school see you as reserved and introverted, while those who met you when you were of college age see you as an egotistical pleasure seeker. Your aunt fits in the first category. You had been an emotional child. Crying over miniscule circumstances, awkward interactions with relatives, and a lack of an interest in sports added to your family's preconceived ideas. "He sure is sensitive," they would say. But you are older now; those times have come and gone.

You are desperately trying to prove that you are not the same little kid you once were. You make it a habit to stop by your aunt's house at least once a month and converse with her so that she might know the real you. But you cannot show her the real you. The real you is wrapped in secrecy, lust, and deceit. You chat with her for hours, and the conversation is pleasant. However, you notice that whenever your uncle asks a question, your aunt is quick to respond on your behalf. She never lets you speak for yourself.

"So where's your girlfriend?" he asks.

"Myles has plenty of time for that sort of thing," she smoothly replies. "He's not even thinking about that right now. Isn't that right, Myles?" She then begins to laugh and shakes her head back and forth. "I'm not gunna know what to do when you get a girlfriend," she chuckles to herself. You smile and assure her that you are only focused on your studies and that girls will come when the time is right. Little does she know you are lying through your teeth.

She need only peek at your phone to discover the sheer magnitude of her misjudgment. She would never dream that beneath his rehearsed smile, her sweet, innocent nephew was fighting a demon no one could see. Somewhere in between your aunt's laughter and your uncle's curiosity, you hear a brief vibration. It is your phone. You pull yourself from the conversation and reach into your pocket. Before you can unlock the screen, your heart stops. You feel completely numb for a split second and then your entire body is flooded with adrenaline.

Not her, not now.

You glance again at the message, hoping it has somehow vanished so that you can continue your day without incident, but it is still there. You had hoped to never see her name on your phone again: Kendra. In the message box underneath her dreadful name are the words, "I'm lonely, come over." Abruptly, and without the slightest bit of consideration for your family, you excuse yourself, kiss your aunt good-bye, and are out the door. You're going sixty in a residential neighborhood—on your way to see Kendra.

Kendra is the type of girl whose only concerns are me, I, and mine. She is the type of girl who sends her boyfriend to the store, then invites you over while he's gone. She's the kind of girl that would rather complain about her problems than make an effort to solve them, the kind of girl who follows people on Twitter just to gossip about them, the kind of girl you don't bring home to mom. She hasn't always been like this. You remember how innocent she was when you two first met. She used to cover her face with a pillow and tell you to change the subject whenever you told her your crazy sex stories. You told her to stay innocent, and you loved her as a person . . . or so you thought. You were living a reckless, lust-driven life but you kept it strictly platonic with her. She was an angel, and you wouldn't dare think of involving her in your disgusting world.

That was until one day when the two of you were lying on the couch in her spare attic, when no one was home. You were watching a low-budget horror movie on Netflix and laughing at how bad the actors were. You made a corny joke that no other girl would laugh at, but she did. In fact, she laughed harder than you had expected her to, so you began to tickle her. "What's so funny, huh? What's so funny?" you repeat playfully as you hold her down and wiggle your fingers across her abdomen. She is hysterical now. You watch her nose crinkle and scrunch up against her face like tinfoil compressed in your palm. You love the way her nose does that. You had always noticed it, but today is the first time you really appreciate how cute it is. There is so much pain and filth in your life: She is your escape.

When you feel she has had enough, you release her and let her catch her breath. "You're crazy," she gasps between huge gulps of air.

"I know," you say, leaning back on the couch.

"I look like a complete idiot. Look at my hair!" she yells, gesturing to the wild brown mane twisted into a messy bun atop her head.

"Your hair always looks like that," you say jokingly. Kendra shoves one of her tiny fists in your face and raises her middle finger.

"Shut up," she says before laying her head on your chest. This is a first. Tickling was one thing, but this was something new. You have been with plenty of girls before her (and they had let you do a lot more than cuddle), but there is something about this embrace that makes you nervous. Flustered, you begin to wonder anxiously if she can feel your heart rate accelerating. Just as you sense your sweat beginning to bead up, the aroma of her conditioner fills your nostrils and calms you.

"You comfortable?" you ask.

"Never been better," she says tenderly. Your eyes meet. Your heart has relocated to your stomach. You wonder how much longer you have until it explodes, but you maintain eye contact. This is something you have never felt before. In this world of hookup apps and sex on the first date, your love life has been reduced to mechanical sensuality and blocked numbers. But this is different, you're sure of it. You both simultaneously move your heads closer until your eyes instinctively close. Then you wait for the fireworks. But they aren't coming. All you feel is the cold embrace of wet lips, followed by a hand getting caught as Kendra attempts to run it through your curly hair. "No, not her too!" you think to yourself, opening your eyes and pulling back. You can tell by the look in her eyes that she is feeling satisfied, and she snuggles up even closer to you before falling asleep.

***

Your reminiscing is cut short when you arrive at Kendra's house. It pains you to remember the way she was before you turned her into a monster. You park in your usual spot (three houses down) and turn the car off. You open the glove box, grab a condom that you won't be using, spray on some cologne, pop a piece of gum into your mouth, and exit your vehicle. As you pace toward the house, you think about how you should have never taken her virginity. If you had known that one night all those years ago would have led you both down this road, you would have never given her that first kiss. Now she is part of your routine, just like all the others. You hate that it has to be this way. You don't want to do it but you have to. You reach the front door, and it's unlocked like it always is. You push it open, and her dogs begin to bark (right on schedule). If they knew what you were about to do to their owner, they would surely attack. Lucky for you they are in crates.

Kendra is upstairs in her room, wearing a sports bra and yoga pants. You both do your best to make small talk and pretend you don't know why you are here. She tells you a story that you aren't listening to concerning some person you don't care about. Your mind is only on one thing. You recall her getting dressed after the first time you guys did it, when she told you that as long as she was alive you could always make love to her. This had excited you—almost as much as when she had asked you to show her your world. She was not the first girl whose virginity you'd stolen, and you doubt she will be the last. They always did the same thing. They give a piece of themselves away to a guy like you, thinking they are in love. Although this had all been new to her, Kendra had completely submitted herself to you and repeatedly told you to do what you pleased. You had talked about everything you were going to do to her and how much she was going to love it, but after the first month you were already out of creative ideas. And quite frankly, you could care less about impressing her. After all, there were others to attend to.

You grow weary of half listening to Kendra's small talk, so you make your move. She is standing in front of her enormous closet, ranting about how she got two rompers for the price of one.

"I didn't come here for that," you say, standing up.

You approach her slowly, gazing down upon her petite frame. You grab her by the neck and kiss it. She expels a soft breath of air and drops the rompers on her carpet. Effortlessly you pick her up and lightly toss her onto the bed. She looks aroused yet slightly fearful. This thrills you, but only for a moment. You go through your routine of sucking, kissing, and slapping until it is ready.

"We have to be quiet," she whispers. "My dad is in the next room. I'll be on top." You lie down, and she climbs on top of you. Staring at her shut door, and with her back facing you, she begins to thrust up and down while using her left hand to cover her own mouth.

Her room is dimly lit; however, her blinds are cracked just enough for some of the moonlight to shine through, illuminating one side of her face. It begins to sicken you. Her face, her stupid face, is forming an expression that makes you want to get up and call the whole thing off. It is not the face of mere pleasure. This is the face someone makes when the person thinks no one else is watching. This is the face of passion and intimacy, neither of which exist between the two of you. "Look at her," you think to yourself. "She actually thinks this means something." You become enraged by this notion, so much so that you forget this is supposed to feel good, and you go limp.

"No, no, no, no, no!" she says frantically, trying to get you back up. "Just a little more." You feel like calling it quits until she eagerly gasps, "I have an idea."

Grasping your giant hand in her small one, Kendra leads you out of her bedroom and across the hallway into the upstairs bathroom.

"Are you crazy?" you ask angrily.

Before you can say anything else, Kendra interrupts you. "Do me in front of the mirror."

You're still angry with her, but the idea turns you on. With your right hand, you grab her by the back of the neck and bend her over the bathroom counter.

"Hurry," she squeaks out, her lips pressed against the white countertop.

But still there is nothing you can do. As you stare at your shirtless reflection in the mirror, you wonder what you are doing with your life. This addiction is controlling you. You wasted all of last semester ditching class and manipulating clueless girls who were looking to you for something that their daddies hadn't given them. You have no job, no goals, no clue. Your life has lost all meaning and sensation. You can't remember the last time you were happy. Your existence has become little more than a waiting period in between meaningless hookups.

You know there has to be more to life than this. You want to stop but cannot, and you spend your days sulking in unfathomable depths of depression, wondering whose heart you'll break this week. This has grown far beyond impressing your friends. Even they wouldn't approve of your behavior. This is a craving that is seemingly beyond your control, and as you stand naked behind Kendra, these thoughts all hit you at once. You have no clue how long you have just been standing there, but you realize it must have been a while. So you pretend you are still interested in the sex and rummage around in her medicine cabinet, searching for any kind of lube. You find a small bottle of scented lotion and begin to apply it. Still nothing.

"Uuugh." Kendra sighs, visibly upset. "Come here." She uses a hand towel to wipe off the lotion, kneels down, and begins bobbing back and forth between your legs.

This does the trick. Kendra pulls you back to her room. Keeping your eyes on her parents' bedroom door, you nakedly tiptoe through another man's house behind his daughter as he sleeps. You remember when Kendra first introduced you to her father. You can recall shaking his hand with the same fingers that had been inside his daughter the night before. You wonder if there is a special place in hell made just for you. Kendra lays on her bed and pulls you on top of her.

"Why do we always have to do it like this?" she groans.

You close your eyes and begin to kiss her (imagining you are with another girl). Kendra rubs your chest and shoulders with one hand while getting you ready with the other. This is how you must always have sex. You must be tricked into it. Before you know it, the familiar sensation envelops your loins, and you hear the faint high-pitched moan women let out during penetration.

You begin to thrust, but you are not even engaged in the moment. You might as well be clocking in for work with the way you are going through the motions. You are doing fine.

However, she is breathing heavy and attempts to grab your shoulder blades. You do not allow it. With one swift motion you pin her arms above her head and bite her neck. This is not love making. There is nothing romantic going on here. You are about to finish when you make the horrid mistake of looking at her face. She looks so content, so passionate. No doubt emotions are running through her mind. Emotions that you will have to deal with when this is over. Her ridiculous expression, you can't stop staring at it. "What did I do wrong?" you wonder. "How can she possibly think this is anything more than sex?"

Furious, bewildered, and completely turned off, you decide you have had enough and pull out.

"What's wrong?" she asks. She looks like she was suddenly awoken from her favorite dream.

"Nothing," you say, not even attempting to sound sincere. "I just have to go." You stand up and begin searching the softly lit room for your clothes.

"Where are you going?" she asks loudly.

"Shut up, you're going to wake him up."

Kendra sits up and slides on her bra. "We are going to talk about this."

You wonder who on earth this crazy girl thinks she is. There's no reason for you to explain anything to her. In the middle of Kendra's half-naked ranting and your fumbling around in the darkness trying to put on pants, your phone vibrates. You almost laugh at the way she pounces on it. You would have gotten to it first if you hadn't had one leg hanging out of your jeans.

"Who the hell is Kalee!" Kendra hisses as she cocks her hand back, getting ready to launch your phone across the room.

Like an imbecile, you hop over to her on one leg and grab her arm just in the nick of time. You snatch your phone away from her, pull up your pants, and exit the room. Kendra is right on your heels muttering curses in your ear as you descend the staircase. As soon as you step outside she wraps a cold tiny hand around your wrist. Your instinct is to pull away, but you hear sniffles. Curious, you turn around to see the woman you once thought you loved with tears streaming down her face. Her makeup is running, and in her haste to chase you out of her house, you notice she has put her yoga pants on inside out. Your sick sense of humor finds this amusing, and you fight to hold back the smile that begins to break through.

"You always do this," Kendra sobs. You stand emotionless as this five-foot-three waste of your time begins to bore you with the same tirade you have heard a thousand times.

"You never call me unless it's to hook up. We never hang out during the day. I've never met your family. You never take me out," . . . blah, blah, blah. Her words begin to blend together until you no longer care enough to comprehend what she is yelling about. If you do this every time, then why is it still a surprise to her? You watch her mouth move: the mouth you once thought was pretty, the mouth you used to long to kiss. She's getting animated now, using all sorts of hand gestures and stomping. She's bound to wake someone up. You stare into her eyes, and for a moment, you try your absolute hardest to care. After all, you two did just have sex. The least you could do is show some empathy. But you cannot. In fact, this situation isn't even on your mind at the moment. All you want to do is reach into your pocket, pull out your phone, and find out what Kalee wanted.

You stand there attempting to force yourself to show some compassion until Kendra finally takes a breath. Then in an indifferent voice, you calmly utter, "Are you done?"

With a scream that has undoubtedly been formed over years of unmet expectations and painful letdowns, Kendra begins to attack you. It doesn't hurt. You cover your soft spots and block most of her wild swings with relative ease. Eventually, she tires herself out, calls you horrible names (all of which you've heard before), walks to her porch, curses at you some more, and finally goes back inside. None of this phases you.

This has all happened before. That's the cycle. You make cheesy, vague promises that you both know you can't keep, followed by her saying she wants to trust you but is afraid of getting hurt again. You ask her to meet you somewhere just to talk about everything, and the rest is history. Nothing changes. She will pretend to be a philosopher on Twitter for a week or two, posting quotes copied from Tumblr on her feed about how happy she is being single, how she is going to better herself, and how the breakup (if you want to call it that) is a blessing.

You know it's all lies. You will repeat this process over the next few months with a new girl, and when it inevitably ends the same way, you will recycle Kendra again like you always have. As you stand outside of her massive house, you remove your phone from your pocket and read Kalee's text message: "I'm only in town a few days. You better stop by before I go back to NorCal." It is 3:30 a.m., but like the addict you are, you actually press the call button. Filled again with the adrenaline rush of anticipation, you sit inside your car, tapping your foot, eagerly hoping she answers. You don't know that someone is watching you and has been the entire time.

Nebulous

Something is off within you. You don't understand why you can't be normal. Life made you like this. It is not your fault you are the way you are. (At least that's what you tell yourself.) In third grade, when most children were only concerned with candy and recess, you and Jenifer (a girl your age) would sneak off to places where eyes could not see (but someone's did). Then you'd touch each other in spots no eight-year-old should ever be touched. You were perplexed by the feelings Jenifer was able to bring out of you. Part of you knew something about it was wrong, but a bigger part of you ached when she was absent from class. Without Jenifer you were alone. You had been an odd child, one who was picked last for everything and sat alone on a step during lunchtime. You watched from a distance as other kids played tag and jump rope. You wanted to ask them if you could join, but you were too afraid. You longed to be acknowledged. The janitor, Mr. Earl, took pity on you and would offer you sticks of licorice from one of his rough, wrinkly, red hands.

You were isolated, and your isolation led to desperation. You became willing to do anything to fit in, anything to call someone your friend. In high school you would bounce back and forth between different groups, trying desperately to look like part of the crowd. On days you didn't feel like pretending, you'd sit by yourself in between two library bookshelves. After your first year of college, you met Jared and Derrick. They are the type of kids who would have bullied you in high school had you known them then. They are the kind of kids who talk about being millionaires but make no effort to move out of their moms' houses. They are the kind of kids who drop out of the school that their parents pay for, because they are content with working for minimum wage, the kind of kids who brag about getting kicked out of clubs.

They don't know about your past, but they seem to share your monstrous sex drive. They introduce you to their crew; it seems like a match made in heaven. Everyone gathers around as you all begin to boast about your sexual prowess, exaggerating any detail possible, hoping to look like the alpha male. Each story is more profane than the last.

In desperate need of a positive male influence, you anxiously count down the days until Ethan returns home from the military. Ethan is three years your senior. You look up to him as a role model and a guide through this complicated journey known as manhood. Ethan was a varsity football quarterback who became a United States Marine. Although you only ever see him briefly in between deployments, you couldn't wait for him to return home and check in on your life's developments. The two of you would engage in late-night conversations about commitment, jobs, sports, girls—anything imaginable. Ethan was Jared's older brother, and although he adored his younger sibling with all his heart, he urged you not to follow in Jared's footsteps. You marveled at how different the two of them were. Ethan did not smoke or drink. He had a long-term girlfriend, whom he cherished, and he always had a plan for where his life was headed. Jared on the other hand was an unemployed party animal who despised his brother's success. He numbed his mind to his pain by drinking, popping, or smoking anything he could get his hands on.

Ethan sees something inside of you that you pretend does not exist. "You have so much potential," he's told you in the past with a firm hand on your shoulder. "So does my brother, but he's convinced himself that he enjoys this life... I can tell that you don't."

Ethan can always see beyond what you're saying. He is difficult to lie to, even over the phone. You remember how nervous you were admitting to him that you had broken your promise of abstaining from sexual intercourse during his absence. Before he had departed, you had acknowledged that you had a problem and had given him your word that you would refrain from having any more meaningless sex. Instead, you would focus on getting to know yourself until he returned. Ethan had patted you on the back and reassured you that he believed in you, only for you to succumb to temptation the very next week. With shaky hands and sweaty palms, you had skated around the issue for an hour before reluctantly admitting that you had failed yet again.

"I know I disappointed you," you whimpered with your head lowered, unable to look Ethan in the eye as you awaited his impending judgment. But judgment never came.

"You fell. We all fall," he uttered somberly. "I see you trying, though. I still have faith in you."

Fighting back tears with all your might, you wondered what Ethan saw in you that allowed him to put up with your perpetual backsliding. This had been the third time you had appeared on his doorstep at an ungodly hour of the night, brokenhearted due to your own self-inflicted wounds. Although Ethan never hesitated to reprimand you if he disapproved of your behavior, he never judged you. He never made you feel stupid. Ethan had pleaded with you not to waste your weekend in San Diego with Jared and Derrick. "You already know what's going to happen down there, Myles," he had said. "Stay home and try to find a job, man."

You had listened attentively to every word Ethan had had to say. By the time he had finished, you had been so fired up and motivated to take charge of your life that you texted Jared and Derrick in a group chat, informing them that you would use the upcoming weekend to search for a job rather than party. As the message was being sent, you felt a weight being lifted off your shoulders, and you were thankful for Ethan's teachings. That was until the guys assaulted your ego with their attacks on your masculinity and crude jokes questioning your sexual orientation. In a pathetic attempt to reestablish your place in the group, you rapidly began to backtrack and before you know it, you are hunched up in the back of Derrick's Lexus on your way to San Diego.

***

You stand behind Jared at the sorority party as he talks to three of the most attractive females you have ever seen in your life. The entire venue smells like weed, and the music is so loud you can barely hear what your friend is saying to the ladies. It doesn't matter. Everyone at the party is only here for one thing. Derrick comes running through the crowd followed by three cookie-cutter surfer boys and yells, "Shots everybody!" You have never had a sip of alcohol before tonight. Jared knows this. He spent the entire drive here giving you a pep talk about relaxing and letting loose. He told you to drink and take whatever was offered to you, because it would make him look bad if you refused. You are desperate not to mess up this friendship; plus you've heard that alcohol helps release tension. Your first shot of tequila feels like you have swallowed a lit match. You try your hardest to hide the pain and look cool. (But you don't.) Derrick gives you a thumbs-up from behind a girl he is dry humping. About four shots in, you begin to realize you have made a terrible mistake. You feel woozy and anxiously search for a place to sit down and gather your thoughts.

Then you remember that Jared told you to always look like you are having fun. Sitting down might make you appear boring. A chubby Caucasian man stumbles across the sticky floor and hands you a bottle of Captain Morgan. "Drink up, bro. I'm done for the night," he says, patting you on the back before exiting the property.

Remembering Jared's instructions, you begin sipping the liquor straight from the nozzle. As you lower the bottle, you notice one of the girls Jared had been talking to earlier is walking toward you. She looks like she has been torn straight out of a Victoria's Secret catalogue. She is about five foot five with a perfect jawline, and her blue eyes are fixated on you as she makes her way over. Her lower abs tease you as they peek out below her crop top, and her white shorts are so tight and small that you're astonished she was even able to put them on. You are still slightly tense, so you take another swig of alcohol to kill your nerves.

She introduces herself as Jackie and asks if she can share your newly acquired bottle of booze. The two of you wind up spending the rest of the night hooking up and getting incoherently drunk. You wake up together the next morning in a bathtub lined with dried orange vomit. Your head is throbbing, and you have no idea where your friends are.

Eventually, you remember that the woman's name is Jackie but only because Jared reminds you of this when you find him outside, dragging Derrick's limp body to the car. It dawns on you that none of you guys can fully piece together the events of the previous night, yet Jared and Derrick celebrate triumphantly, ironically referring to the weekend as "one to remember." Soon after, you would get so drunk during a kickback at Derrick's house that you would wake up in a pair of black basketball shorts that were not your own. When you asked how you got into someone else's pants, Derrick informed you that you had been so plastered that you had urinated on yourself, and he and Jared had taken it upon themselves to change you.

On a different occasion, you drank yourself into such a sloppy frenzy that a pudgy, cake-faced girl with bad breath took advantage of you in your altered state. You remember coming to your senses halfway through the encounter and pushing her aside, but not before Jared caught the whole thing on video. You then spent at least twenty minutes the next morning attempting to brush the taste of halitosis off of your tongue.

Although every weekend you spent with Jared and Derrick had been eventful, and everyone laughed when you told them your stories, you never truly felt like one of them, and you secretly wondered if this was all there was to life. You try your hardest to ignore this feeling, but it persists. Regardless of how much you fake it or which girl you're seeing at the moment, you know that something is off about the way you are living, and this keeps you up at night.

Perhaps you've realized how deeply your mother would disapprove of everything you're doing. Your mother, your sweet mother, she was your first friend. She had been the only one who was there for you during your times of need. Like static you had clung to her, relying on her for anything and everything. She had been your world. In fact, her influence on you had been so strong that you had even taken on some of her personality traits. You had inherited her compassion and sense of humor as well as adopted her apprehensions and inhibitions. It would take you years to fully shake off her negativity, so in the meantime you had decided to mask them with bravado and lust. You remember slamming a fellow student's head into the pavement for likening your mother's physical appearance to that of an ape before ultimately losing the fight when his friends came to his rescue. So as you continue your journey of abusing and mistreating women, you are haunted by the fact that you are a walking contradiction.

The concentrated, undying love shared between mother and son is not reflected in the way you treat the opposite sex. You remember spending hours of your time rehearsing how you were going to tell Samantha you liked her. The two of you had never been on a date. Actually, you had never worked up the courage to start an actual conversation with her. She was the only seventh grader in your gym class who seemed nice enough to approach. Her friend Vivica had made a fool of you in Spanish class. She had let you borrow a pencil, prompting someone to joke that she must have a crush on you. In a frantic attempt to protect her image, Vivica had made sure to loudly assert that you were ugly and that the two of you would never date in a million years. Incidents such as this had not been uncommon for you. Your fearful, quiet persona, coupled with the constant suppression of a voracious and premature sexual appetite, had made you seem strange, therefore making you a magnet for ridicule.

Denial and persecution had closed you off from interacting with other students, so you retreated to the surreal fantasy-land of books and your own imagination. But Samantha wasn't like the other girls. She never called you ugly or laughed when the popular kids insulted you. You would sit on the rail by the lockers after class and watch her interact with those around her. You were mesmerized by her and would watch enviously as boys with more confidence than you asked if they could help her carry her overstuffed pink backpack to the car. A few times she caught you staring at her and sent a smile back in your direction. Not knowing how to react, you'd let go of the rail to wave back, only to immediately grasp it again, catching yourself before you fell to the ground. You thought there had to be a reason she smiled at you, and then in your nervousness you'd rub your sweaty palms on your jeans. "Today is the day. You can do it," you'd repeatedly tell yourself.

This time, when the bell rings, you wait for Samantha to come around the corner. When she is within earshot you make the mistake of calling her over to where you are seated on the rail. Multiple heads turn.

"What could this kid possibly want with Samantha?"

In a voice that is fighting a losing battle against nervous-ness, you timidly tell her that you think she is really pretty. Lacking the boldness to finish the rest of what you had planned to say, you awkwardly await her response. Laughter has erupted in the area, and even though there are only about twelve kids around you, it feels like the entire world is looking at you. Torn between the children's laughter and her pity for you, Samantha turns to her friends, who chime in comments like "Eww" and "Come on Sam, let's go." Samantha looks back at you, then at her friends, before walking away without saying a word.

Later, you would hear her in the hallway, gossiping about how creepy and weird you were. Over the years, you would inadvertently develop a callus over your heart to protect it from feeling any more disappointment. As you grew from a boy into a man, you distanced yourself from those who had known you in your youth. The more you matured physically, the more you began to meet new women: women who pursued you, women who found you attractive and mysterious, women who thought they could change you.

Jared taught you how to talk to females, and Derrick reassured you that it was okay to release your pent-up testosterone to its fullest extent. You look to them for the guidance you pretend not to need from your own father, and you are grateful for their lessons. You watch as Derrick insults, cheats, and parties his way into multiple women's pants. He says the most vulgar, disrespectful things to them—things your mother told you never to say. He is sexually aggressive and does not hide his intentions in the slightest, yet time and time again, women desire some form of commitment from him. "They want what they can't have," he tells you. Derrick is successful with his approach but only with a certain type of girl. Jared is the one you should pay more attention to.

Jared has a past he never talks about and a slyness that makes you uneasy. He is quick to tell you how one of your relationships will end before it even starts and is usually correct in his assessment. He is a master manipulator. Unlike Derrick, Jared's intentions with women are unclear. You have seen him lie without breaking eye contact. He will tell a girl he loves her and then let her best friend go down on him. You have watched Jared get caught in a lie and talk his way out of any responsibility for his actions. Jared is the one who pressured you into not using condoms anymore and finishing on women's bellies. He is cold, calculating, and methodical. He will spend days, sometimes even weeks, studying a girl's social media accounts, analyzing what she posts and learning as much as he can about her personality before he approaches her. He can talk to entire groups of women by himself and have them all eating out of his palm. He is charming and intimidating. He even intimidates you. But Jared has taken you under his wing. He can completely reconfigure your brain and change your way of thinking.

He strips the emotion out of everything. He only deals with things as they are. Jared does not hope; he does not dream. You wonder if he even feels. He despises questions that start with "What if" or "I wonder." He says he only deals in absolutes, whatever that means. The two of you used to butt heads, because you were a dreamer and he was a realist. You used to write poetry that you kept in a shoebox underneath your bed, but you have since stopped writing. Jared says the likelihood of your poetry ever becoming notable is next to zero and advises you not to waste your time. It pains you to cut emotion from your life, but you notice that Jared never gets hurt like you do. You have seen Derrick cry once or twice but never Jared. Now you cannot remember the last time you went on an actual date. You don't recall the last time you closed your eyes for a kiss or what it feels like to hold hands or introduce a girl to your mother. As your stack of numbers grows, your humanity shrinks, and you feel completely void and indifferent—that is, until you meet Jane.

Jane

You are an island, surrounded on all sides by a sea of loneliness. You have no visitors other than the unlucky women who find themselves stranded in your presence. Like anyone who is marooned, they search you for nourishment. You possess none. You will not take them to expensive restaurants or pull out their chairs. You will not ask them about their dreams or make yourself available in times of crisis. You will not share any intimate moments together. Your connection is purely physical. Marcy was one of the lucky ones. The two of you met through a mutual friend. He informed you that Marcy found you attractive and particularly charming. This was no surprise. Making your prey feel comfortable was your specialty. You remember how hard she laughed the day the two of you first met when you playfully bent down on one knee, pretending to ask for her hand in marriage.

"You're crazy," she gasped, covering her mouth in shock. "All these people are looking."

You did this with every girl. You would wait until they revealed something minor that the two of you had in common before joking that it must have been "meant to be." Audacious public gestures like this always made them laugh and gave you a chance to show off your phony confidence. Marcy was twenty-two, and you were nineteen. She constantly brought attention to the age difference between you with remarks like "You're just a baby" and "Look at you trying to act like a big boy." But she dated you all the same. The two of you had gone out twice in your city, but you had gotten no more than a kiss. This troubled you to no end. Jared told you that it was because she was older.

"Older girls don't want to have to drive to you. Go out to her city next time, and I guarantee those panties will drop."

That night, Marcy texts you that she is getting off work at nine and asks if she should come see you afterward. You eagerly inform her that you will drive out to her city, pick her up from work, and take her out. She responds well, and you can tell by the look on her face when she climbs into your 4Runner that you are on the right track. She had gotten off later than expected, so most restaurants in her area were closed, except Denny's. In a voice that sounds genuinely contrite, you pretend to beat yourself up over your inexperience at planning dates.

"I wanted to take you someplace better," you say, dramatically running a hand through your curls and doing your best to appear upset. "If you still want to eat, I'm down. If not, I understand." Secretly you're hoping she isn't hungry so that you can save your money.

Marcy looks at the Denny's and then back at you. You can see the concern written on her face. You realize that she's really buying your little act. "Let's just get a smoothie or something," she says, rubbing your arm. "It's fine, I promise."

You pay for both smoothies, and she cannot stop smiling. Set the bar low, and anything that follows will be an improvement. It's getting late now, and the two of you walk through the empty parking lot back to your car. Your mind is racing. You are searching for an unilluminated space to park in so that you can get what you came here for, but then Marcy decides to break the silence with a stupid question.

"Out of all the girls you could be with, why are you with me?" You hate such questions. You hate questions that force you to lie.

You want to answer, "Because I have an insatiable desire to sleep with as many females as possible, and I'm hoping that the seven dollars and fifty cents I just spent on these smoothies wasn't for nothing." But instead you calmly turn to her and reply, "Because I've never met anyone like you before."

You had more to say, but before you are able to dig into your bag of repetitious, overused clichés, Marcy interrupts you. "Aww, that's so sweet," she says with a content smile.

You stop walking about twenty feet away from your car, turn, and kiss her gently before pulling back. You make sure it appears that hooking up is not on your mind. "I should probably be getting you back home," you say, unlocking both your front and rear doors.

"Drop me off at my car. It's back where I work," Marcy says, climbing into the passenger seat. As you pull into the JCPenny parking lot, you notice she is being uncharacteristically quiet.

"Here we are," you say with a smile, pulling in next to Marcy's black Mazda 6. "I had a great time hanging out with you. I hope I get to see you soon." You make it a point to totally ignoring Marcy's flustered demeanor.

"Is that it?"

"What do you mean?" you ask, pretending to be confused.

Marcy turns to face you now, not even bothering to unclip her seatbelt. "You haven't been affectionate at all tonight. You pulled back when we were at Denny's, and now you're going to say bye without kissing me?

"Last time we hung out you could barely keep your hands off me. What's wrong?"

This is the response you had been hoping for. You have been busy subconsciously sowing seeds of confusion all night, and she has finally brought the right topic up. Marcy has blown her cover; she has shown her hand. In a lie told so confidently that you almost believed it yourself, you explain to Marcy that you do like her but you are afraid of going too far and that you don't want to put her in a position where she feels uncomfortable. There is a brief silence that seems to last a lifetime. Your adrenaline skyrockets as you await her response. This is why you do it. You crave this feeling: the feeling of breaking down someone's walls, the feeling of bending a person to your will. It intoxicates you.

"I've never had anybody say anything like that to me in my entire life," Marcy finally confides in a shaky voice.

A delightful feeling of success engulfs your body. She has bought it. Marcy begins to riff about her arbitrary trust issues and how amazing you are. You let her talk herself silly, already imaging Jared and Derrick's faces when they hear you banged a twenty-two-year-old. When she's done ranting, you convince her that you are nothing like her exes and that you are sincerely interested in getting to know her as a person. You lean in to kiss her on the cheek, but she grabs your face and presses her soft lips onto yours. Marcy takes charge, the way you always expected an older woman would. Your tongues intertwine in a dance of deceitful passion while her mitten-covered hands glide across your chest.

Before you can get yourself properly situated, Marcy unbuckles her seatbelt and gently bites your bottom lip, pulling it out a little before whispering, "Let's go in the back."

The engine is still running, but without hesitation, you unclip your seatbelt and rush to the rear driver's-side seat of your car. This is going even better than you'd hoped. You leap into the back, and almost instantaneously Marcy is there. Climbing on top of you, her straight white teeth sink into the tendons of your neck, releasing a chill down your spine. You pull her blouse over the top of her head and toss it in the front seat. As the windows begin to fog around you, you plant kisses on her chest and belly. You run your hands up her back toward her bra, but before you can undo it, Marcy violently pushes you back.

"Wait, we can't do this!" she shrieks while still sitting in your lap.

You want to pay attention, but there is no blood in your brain at the moment. So instead you stare in silent confusion at one of the most vexing women you have ever dated.

"What's wrong?" you ask, more angry than concerned.

"I'm sorry," Marcy gasps. Her enormous bosom is rising and falling rapidly as she attempts to catch her breath. "I just still have a lot of questions about you. I can't put my finger on it, but there's something about you that scares me. It's like everything you say has been . . . rehearsed."

Stunned, you rack your brain to find something to say that might give her some solace. You can't come up with anything. It's clear you won't be getting any further with Marcy tonight, and you no longer wish to continue this facade, so you bluntly say, "Maybe you should go."

You watch as Marcy curses you out in Spanish and angrily collects her purse. She reaches into the front seat and snatches her top. You watch disappointedly as her blouse stretches over her massive breasts, covering up what you almost had. You watch her speed out of the empty JCPenny parking lot and turn the corner. You feel nothing. Then you calmly reach for your phone and check the time: 2:20 a.m. You also see that you have a new text message from Katie.

"Are we still on for next Friday?"

***

Katie is nothing like Marcy. She is eighteen and has never known her father. Her mother did the best she could to raise her and pay the bills, but in her haste to earn a living she had neglected to teach her daughter to have standards when it comes to boys. Katie is the type of girl you prey on. Due to her father's absence and her mother's workaholic personality, Katie's only influences are social media and the music she listens to. She's grown to despise her mother for always being at work and blames her for all the pain in her life. Since childhood she has been called a good girl, and she longs to abandon this image. She is book smart and could have straight A's if she applied herself more, but she pretends to think that school is useless and posts videos of herself vaping and drinking alcohol so that everyone can see that she is cool.

Katie is attracted to the crowd you act like you belong to and the image associated with guys like you. She knows nothing about men, besides what her friends say about them. She lacks the conversational skills to keep them interested, so she prides herself in getting male attention in other ways. She frequently posts pictures of her half-naked body across her various social media accounts. Although she acts like it gets on her nerves, she discretely enjoys ignoring the droves of men who post provocative comments about her photos. Girls like Katie are a dime a dozen. Katie is a virgin, but she talks to you like an escort. She seems experienced based on her text messages, but once you meet her in person, you quickly dissect her disguise and realize that the poor girl has no idea what she has gotten herself into.

Eager to impress you, she lets you sleep with her the night the two of you meet. You remember opening your eyes to discover the expression of sheer terror and intense pain written all over the face of your latest victim. You can recall the familiar arm of misery draping across your shoulder as you peeled off the bloody condom, realizing that you had stolen yet another human being's innocence. Katie became attached to you and made the mistake of showing up at your new job with her friends. There she was met coldly with a look in the opposite direction, as if the two of you had never met. That was the last you ever saw of her. Jane knew about these stories. She knew about Kendra, Marcy, and Katie. She knew about the sorority party and Kalee. She knew it all, and she did not judge you. Perhaps worst of all, she knew about Cassie.

Cassie is the girl who feels even less than you do. She is just as damaged as you and even nastier than you could ever be. Cassie is the girl that baptized you into this way of life. She was technically the third girl you were intimate with but the first that you were able to finish in. Cassie was known for getting around and being kinky in the sheets. You were first introduced to her at a kickback in your friend's backyard, where you noticed her in the Jacuzzi, tongue kissing and straddling an acquaintance of yours. You recall the way she looked you up and down as you walked past her.

"That girl doesn't know the meaning of faithful," muttered Conner, one of your friends at the gathering. "Stay away from her, bro." But of course you didn't listen and found yourself parking at the golf course beneath her house before walking half a mile up a steep hill to her apartment complex, where she was waiting for you behind an unlocked door.

You remember her taking control, introducing you to various positions and reinventing the way you ate certain desserts. You recall cautiously sneaking into your mother's room and scooping large wads of Vaseline into a plastic baggie. You celebrated triumphantly as you hid the bag in your glove box. You can recollect towering over Cassie as she knelt before you in doggy style. You would spread her apart with your thumbs and pack her anus full of petroleum jelly. She was the only girl who let you do this, and you began to develop a fetish for the way it clenched up and sealed you in. Jared and Derrick barely believed the stories you'd tell them about Cassie, and you didn't blame them. Honestly, you wouldn't have believed them either if the shoe had been on the other foot. That lasted until you introduced her to Derrick. Then he wholeheartedly concurred that your stories must be true.

You always had this unshakeable feeling that Cassie was seeing other people. Her sex drive was too ravenous to be contained by one man, and you were basically a novice, just beginning to develop your skill set. You would soon find out that Derrick was one of her many other partners and that the two were planning on filming a sex tape together. Jane knows all of this, and it does not bother her. You poured your heart out to her the night at the park when the two of you met under the moonlight, because you were finally ready to open up. You were being torn apart by apathy and haunted by nightmares before you finally agreed to share your past with her.

You told her everything. You let her see your soul. Jane had to pry at first, but eventually you spoke openly about third grade, the school bullying, Jared and Derrick, and every girl you had ever been with, from Cassie to Kendra. You explained how it all affected you and made you a monster. You told her you had never wanted to be this way and about how horrible of a person you had become. You let it all out. At times you felt like changing the subject, but there was something about the way she held you that made you keep going. Jane's big brown eyes gleamed with concern as she listened to every word you uttered. You expected her to leave, but her grip never loosened. When you finally finished talking, you felt a sudden sense of fear. You had made yourself vulnerable, something Jared had told you never to do.

You sat in silence, waiting for Jane to speak. When she finally does, you cannot believe your ears. With tears in her eyes, she explains that she is a recovering sex addict as well. She tells you about the way her innocence was stripped from her as a seventh grader and how her heightened desire for intimacy had caused her to spread herself thin, just like you. She explains that like you, she ran with a group of friends who were negative influences on her, driving her to drugs and more sex. Like you, she has an overly protective mother and a father who she is not as close with as she would like to be, and like you, she has always wanted more for herself but didn't know where to look for it. Your emotions are at an all-time high, and you cannot recall the last time you felt this connected with someone. "I'm not the only one," you think. "Someone gets me." With your right hand, you place your thumb and index finger below Jane's chin and lift her sobbing face.

"You are amazing," you whisper. Words cannot express how great it feels to be authentic for once.

"So are you," she utters back. The two of you close your eyes, and as you lean in for a kiss, you agonize over the possible results.

"Please don't let her be like all the others, please."

Your eyes are closed, and you seem to be leaning in for an eternity. Your entire life flashes by: all the letdowns, all the pain you've caused. You think of Kendra's teary-eyed rant and Marcy's justified skepticism. You think of Cassie's pleasure-over-everything outlook on life and how you adopted it from her. You think about all the time you've spent chasing girls you had nothing in common with and wonder how you ended up here on this night with this gem. "What did I do to deserve a present like this?" you ponder as you continue to lean forward. The two of you had met in a familiar way. You had stopped by a sandwich shop on your way home from work. Too impatient to wait in the drive-through, and in a hurry to get home, you had run into the shop with your uniform still on.

Despite both of you being in uniform, there had been something magnetic about the way in which your eyes had met. She had taken your order, and her gaze had never left you, even as she fumbled with the buttons on the screen in front of her. You had gotten her number and taken her out, but there was something about Jane that stopped you from including her in your routine. There was an aura that surrounded her, an aura that made you want to get to know her as a person, not just get in her pants. The two of you had connected. She was easy to talk to and constantly pressured you to open up to her. Tonight was the night you had finally given in to her request, and your lips met as the two of you sat on the park bench in the moonlight. Her soft, moist lips tasted of cotton candy lip gloss, and a new sensation gripped your entire body. As your mouths pressed together, a warm electric buzz began to circulate beneath your skin before making its way through the layers of scar tissue encasing your heart. For a moment, time stood still. Crickets ceased their chirping and frogs their ribbiting. Even the wind took a break from howling and gave you two this moment of peace.

You could have sat there all night kissing her, but your moment of bliss is interrupted by Jane pulling back. The moonlight illuminates her expression. Her face summarizes what you feel, and the two of you can do nothing but stare passionately at each other. You cannot believe that this is what you have been missing out on all this time, and you decide to speak first.

"I'll always be here for you," you say looking into her eyes.

"So will I," she says reassuringly as she shivers from the cold. Forsaking Jared's teachings, you rip off your hoodie and wrap it around Jane; the cold air is now nipping at your forearms.

"Thank you," she utters tenderly as she lays her head on your chest. The two of you silently hold each other beneath the stars for hours until you reluctantly bring up how late it is and the fact that she should be heading home soon.

"I don't want to go," she says, rubbing a smooth, tiny finger over one of your calluses.

"I don't want you to go either," you say sadly. "But we both know it's about that time." With much more hesitation than necessary, the two of you stand up and walk hand in hand, like two long-time lovers, to where your cars are parked.

"I have to pee," she giggles.

You'll never forget that giggle; it will haunt you for months. You remember laughing harder than you had ever laughed with a girl as you watched Jane squat at 3:30 in the morning to pee in a bush. She was so goofy, so full of life, so free.

The two of you would drag out your good-byes for another thirty minutes. They're full of enough kisses, promises, and "I'll miss yous" to make anyone who has ever been heartbroken sick. You finally let her go, and the two of you drive off in separate directions. You can hardly sleep that night and instead spend the time thinking of creative ways to ask Jane to be your girlfriend the next time you see her. Little did you know there would not be a next time. You would wake up the next morning to a text message from Jane stating that she thought things were moving too fast and that she was not ready for a serious relationship. You would later discover through Instagram that she had ditched you for an ex-boyfriend. This was the catalyst that drove you deeper into your addiction than ever before. It was also at this moment that the stranger who had been watching you through all your endeavors decided to make his move.

Favor

"Where is she?" you ask yourself as you rock back and forth on a rusty black swing, attempting to kill some time. "She's never this late."

It has been nearly three months since you and Kendra last spoke to each other, and she has finally broken down and replied to your text message. Just as you predicted she would. She agreed to meet you at the park to talk everything over, but as you sway to and fro on the abandoned swing set under the dim glow of the moonlight, you begin to grow impatient. The sting of Jane's absence is still fresh, and you cannot wait for Kendra to arrive to fill that void. But deep down you know that she can never fill it. You know that all the meaningless sex in the world cannot take the place of true intimacy, and the idea that you are about to manipulate your way into another no-win situation makes you sick to your stomach. The thrill is gone. There is no chase, no excitement. You already know how this story is going to end. This is just something you have to do.

In the midst of your overanalyzing, you hear the crunch of woodchips beneath feet, followed by a strong voice uttering the words, "It doesn't have to be like this, you know."

Startled, you violently whip your head to your right and see an old man leaning on the railing adjacent to you. His hair is knotted and white as snow. He is dressed in a white robe that cascades from his shoulders down to his sandaled feet.

His left palm is wrapped around a wooden cane, and his eyes glow like the flicker of an ember.

"Who are you?" you ask, bewildered at the stranger's unusual appearance.

There is a brief pause as the stranger stares off into the distance before his lips begin to curl into a smile. "I am you. I am who you could be if your feelings didn't control you. I'm who you could be if you stopped wasting so many people's time. I am the voice in the back of your head that tells you that you are better than what your life has produced. I am the reason you never fit in."

You are more confused than you have ever been, and you don't know who this ridiculous old man is or where he has come from, but before you can say anything, he speaks again. "I have been watching you from afar your entire life . . . and I can't say I am pleased with your results."

The old man clearly had more to say, but you have heard enough. "You don't know a thing about me, freak!" you interject angrily. "I've never seen you before tonight, so I'd appreciate it if you would just leave me alone and go back to wherever it is you came from."

The old man chuckles quietly to himself before looking you directly in the eyes. "Your name is Myles Wayne. You were born September 27, 1994, to Sheeran and Barry Wayne. You have one brother who is three years your junior. All your life you have sought to fit in somewhere. Jared and Derrick provided access to the crowd you were excluded from as a child, as well as a means to unleash your sensual eroticism, and you are at this park tonight hoping to parley Kendra back into your dishonest arms."

Rendered speechless for a second time, you can do nothing other than stare in amazement at this peculiar old man as he stares back at you. You wanted to write him off as a crazy old geezer that had happened to accidently wander through the park at 2 a.m. spouting gibberish, but there is something about the look in his eyes and the accuracy with which he speaks that quivers the marrow in your bones.

"How can you possibly know all that?" you finally ask in a shaky voice.

Using his cane to distribute his weight, the old man hobbles over to the swing closest to you and slowly lowers himself into sitting position before resting his cane against the swing set's blue support beam.

"Like I said," he whispers, extending a long, bony arm out and resting his aged hand on your shoulder, "I've been watching you."

You want to flee, but there is a certain magnetism about the stranger's presence that captivates your interest. As he sits next to you with his red eyes piercing you and his hand cupping your left shoulder blade, you have no choice but to listen to what he has to say.

"Before you entered this world, I was here. When you were ostracized by your peers, I saw you. When your pillow was wet with tears of lonesome despair, I noted each one. I have documented every minute of your life down to this very moment, and now it is my time to intercede."

You come to the conclusion that whoever this man is, he must be telling the truth. You know this whether you want to believe him or not. The things he knows are too specific to be lies. Suddenly, the surrealness of the moment is interrupted by a realization. Your mood sways from awe to anger.

"What about my mother?" you say, brushing the old man's hand off your shoulder and raising your voice. "Why did she have to suffer! Why did you not intervene then?"

You recall peacefully watching television while home alone one evening—the evening before everything changed. You remember your father bursting through the door behind your mother, who was weeping profusely. She fell into a heap on one of the kitchen chairs. Between your mother's sobbing and her heartfelt pleas of "Please God!" and "Why me?" you listened as your father woefully explained to you that the only woman you've ever loved has just become a cancer patient. You recall her countless surgeries and trips to the hospital. You cannot erase the image of her lying across the couch unable to move on her own from your mind or the fear that darts through her eyes to this very day whenever she even hears the word cancer.

"What kind of monster would let someone suffer like that?" you ask in disgust.

"Perhaps the same type of monster who would take a virgin's innocence just to boast about it to his friends," the old man replies solemnly. "Perhaps the type of monster who is so absorbed in his own fleshly endeavors that he has learned to completely disregard anyone's feelings other than his own. Perhaps the type of monster who is at this park tonight with the intentions of hurting someone whom he used to claim to love.

"You take advantage of the weak, my child, because you devalue yourself. As for your mother, has her suffering all been in vain?"

Before you can reply to this question, you think back to all the lives your mother's story has touched. You think of the seminars, classes, and awareness walks she attended. You recall witnessing how many other women were able to gather enough strength to keep fighting, knowing that your mother had survived what they were going through. You admire her strength and resilience, the way she used her pain to touch others who were hurting.

It is at this moment that you receive a text message from Kendra: "I'm here in the parking lot. I see your car but not you. Where are you?"

"Let me help you," the stranger utters compassionately, extending his hand to you. "You know there is a better way."

With the distinct and bitter tinge of regret, you reject the stranger's offer and begin to make your way back up to the parking lot. "Please," the old man pleads as the distance between the two of you grows.

"Leave me alone!" you snap harshly, not even bothering to turn back around. "I don't need any help. I've made it this far on my own. I know what I'm doing."

The old man speaks once more before you turn the corner and ascend the stairs to the parking lot. "You've been doing things your own way all your life, Myles. Have you anything to show for it?"

You reach the top of the steps and maneuver to Kendra's sedan. As you climb into the passenger seat, you notice her car is unusually clean. Normally, when she arrives just to talk, her car is a mess, littered with makeup, textbooks, and empty water bottles. But today there is actually enough room for your feet to rest comfortably. The only time you've known her to clean her car was in anticipation of you having sex in the front seat. Kendra looks especially worn-out and low on sleep.

She looks defeated, somehow even more than she normally does.

"Your car is actually clean for once," you joke, attempting to lighten the somber mood. "I can finally put my feet down." But Kendra does not laugh. She does not even attempt to force a fake smile. "What's—"

"I already know what you're going to say, Myles," Kendra interrupts. "We go through this every time."

You are perplexed and somewhat worried about what Kendra is about to say, and for the first time in years, you listen intently to every word she speaks.

"Look, I know you don't like me," she says softly, rapidly blinking to avoid the oncoming tears. "I've known that for a while. I tried to ignore it, but it's obvious. Things will never be like they were in the past." Blinking proves itself to be ineffective, and one long stream of moisture falls rapidly from her left eye as her voice becomes hoarse. Using her sleeve to wipe away the evidence, Kendra continues on.

"I don't care if you like me or not. I just want to have you in my life." Kendra rubs one of her tiny hands back and forth across your upper thigh, moving toward your groin. "So if you want to hook up, we can. You don't have to stay after, and I won't pressure you to take me out anymore. I just want you to be in my life."

With remorse coursing through your bloodstream, you remove your bottoms and recline in Kendra's passenger seat while she climbs on top of you and begins to rise up and down, burying her damp face in your right shoulder. The two of you intertwine in silence, and as you stare out her driver's-side mirror, you think about Jane and the conversation with the stranger. You wonder if he is watching you right now. You think about the girl you are apathetically making love to and how far south she has fallen. You acknowledge that you made her this way. You have broken her.

She has become so desperate to feel a connection with a human being that she has settled for a link that is purely physical. But you are not a human being. At least, you don't feel like one. You have become something less: a carnal creature, a lifeless being whose only escape from madness is sexual promiscuity. Both of you are void inside, and as you stare out the window, a single tear escapes your right eye before splashing in Kendra's hair. When it is over, the two of you go your separate ways without so much as a good-bye hug or a "See you later." She just calmly tells you to call her the next time you feel lonely before driving off into the night.

As you start your car, you begin to hear a faint knocking in the background. At first, you wonder if there is something wrong with your engine, but the noise does not cease as you pull into your driveway and shut off your vehicle. That night you toss and turn, unable to stop thinking about the old man and the conversation that the two of you had on the swing set. Who was he? How did he know so much about you? The knocking would persevere for two weeks. It is not loud enough for you to see a doctor, especially since you have plenty more to worry about, but it does concern you. Ever so softly, it persists.

For fourteen days, you are haunted by the old man's face, followed by the discreet knocking that does not stop. You keep all this to yourself, just like you do with everything else. You cannot stop seeing his face. His piercing red eyes, curly mane, and heavy compassionate voice replay over and over in your consciousness. All the while, the knocking remains constant.

The last thing the stranger said is tormenting you most of all: "Have you anything to show for it?" You think long and hard about your life and what it has produced. Pain, heartbreak, lust, addictions—these are the only words that come to mind. It terrifies you to really think about the old man's question, but your curiosity snatches you out of your comfort zone and drags you back into self-analysis.

When you can no longer deny the facts, you decide to confront your addiction head-on. Scrolling through your phone, you type a message to Jamie, informing her that the two of you need to talk and asking her to come over to your place when she is off of work. You met Jamie on a hookup app where you matched based on physical attraction alone. The two of you went on one date, where you quickly found out that you shared nothing in common other than the mutual feeling of sexual tension. It was then that you established a mutual friends-with-benefits relationship, casually sleeping together whenever it was convenient. Jamie would call you when she was bored or after a bad breakup. You remember the way her palms would bounce off the roof of the white BMW that her daddy bought her in exchange for his absence.

Jamie is uninterested in anything that is not designer, and her lips always taste of iced coffee or booze. You despise who she is as a person and everything she represents, but her outer beauty and masochistic self-indulgence make her almost irresistible to you. But tonight was different. You have invited her over when you are going to be home alone as usual, but this time sex is not on your agenda. Ever since your meeting with the stranger, you have been building up the courage to take control of your flesh, and you have decided to start tonight. You watch from your bedroom window as Jamie exits her Beamer and strolls across the street to your front door. You push the persistent knocking to the back of your mind and head downstairs to let her in. "You can do this," you whisper to yourself as you turn the handle and pull your door open.

"We have to hurry," Jamie says, entering the house with her shoes still on like she owns the place. "I told my mom I was just stopping by the store after work."

Jamie grabs your hand, attempting to lead you up the stairs to your bedroom, but you do not budge. "What's wrong weirdo?" she asks puzzled. "Didn't you hear me say we don't have much time?"

"I texted you saying we needed to talk," you reply, pulling your hand from Jamie's grip.

There is a slight pause as Jamie stands, mouth agape, attempting to gauge how far you are willing to take this joke. But it's not a joke. "When you said you wanted to talk I didn't know you actually meant you wanted to talk," Jamie says, taking a seat on a step. "What could we possibly have to talk about?"

"Us," you say reluctantly. This is the first time you have ever talked your way out of sex.

"There is no us." Jamie laughs, undoing her scarf and exposing her soft, unprotected neck.

Your pulse quickens, and your eyes quickly dart away from her. "That's exactly my point," you say, clenching your fist. "There isn't an 'us,' and that's why I think we should stop seeing each other."

Jamie just stares at you in bewilderment. You had no idea how she was going to react, but it feels good to get that off your chest. You begin to feel a surge of power building inside you.

"You can't be serious." Jamie says this in a voice that indicates she is clearly not used to being denied.

"I am," you state plainly.

"Wow," Jamie scoffs, collecting her purse and scarf. "I can't believe I drove all the way over here just for that. How pathetic."

She stands to leave. You do nothing. You do not chase after her or try to stop her. You do not even open the door to let her out. A victorious feeling of success flows through your entire body as you watch Jamie angrily storm past you and pull back your door handle. You think of how proud Ethan would be. However, your celebration is cut short when you make the mistake of glancing at her backside. In slow motion, you study the way Jamie's perfectly tapered jeans hug her thighs. You think of how nobody is home and how alone you were before she had stopped by. You imagine her lying under you, pinned down beneath your torso, and before you can stop yourself, your arm reaches out and grabs her by the wrist.

"One more time," you utter quietly.

Jamie stops in the open doorway, staring at you like the two of you have never met before. "What is your issue today?" she asks angrily.

She begins to rant about how weird you are and how far she drove to be here. You half listen, knowing that the mere fact that she is still arguing with you means that she is interested. It's a thirty-minute drive back to her house, and Jamie craves sex just as much as you do. She's not going anywhere.

You interrupt her complaining and ask her, "Are you down or not?"

Jamie slowly walks back into your house, swearing under her breath as you eagerly shut the door behind her. "You're an idiot. All you did was waste the little bit of time that we do have," she mutters as you follow her up the steps. "This has to be quick."

You pull off her blouse and unbuckle her jeans, but as things begin to progress between the two of you, you notice that the thumping in your head is growing louder.

After you've stripped each other completely naked, you flip her on her belly and begin to thrust. But the noise keeps on increasing. In an effort to ignore the knocking, you open your eyes and try to focus on Jamie. Her back is arched and her body is rocking back and forth, yet you can't help noting how her heavy breathing is drowned out by the outrageous pounding going on in your head. The deeper you plunge, the louder it gets. Your eardrums are saturated with the sound of thumping, and your mind can no longer focus on anything but the noise.

"Why'd you stop?" Jamie asks, turning around on her hands and knees to check on you. However, you do not see her face looking back at you. All you see is the face of the old man, his intense red eyes penetrating your soul. The knocking grows louder.

"Make it stop!" you scream, grasping your head in your hands before falling to the floor. "Can't you hear it?"

But Jamie cannot hear it. By now she has fearfully collected her clothes and is running half naked through the hallway and down the steps toward the front door.

"Somebody help me!" you scream in agony as the volume of the knocking continues to escalate. Amidst the pounding in your ears, you realize that you have to find the old man.

Michael Wade

Unable to stand, you fumble around on the floor, working your naked body into a pair of basketball shorts before crawling on your stomach into the hallway. Like a maniac, you slide headfirst down the carpeted steps, receiving rug burns all across your abdomen and chest. You grab your car keys and army crawl through your garage. Mustering up all the strength you have left, you pull yourself into your car and speed to the park up the street.

By the time you arrive at the park, your headache has subsided just enough for you to walk. Every move you make causes your skull to pound more severely as you awkwardly stumble down the steps toward the swing set. When you arrive, you collapse face-first into some of the woodchips.

"What do you want from me!" you yell as tears stream down your face. The pain is unbearable now, and the knocking has accelerated to a more rapid tempo.

"I want you," utters a calm voice. You open your eyes to see the stranger towering over you as the knocking in your head ceases. "I want to see you rise to your full potential," he says empathetically while kneeling down beside you in the dirt. "There are treasures hidden within you begging to be unlocked." With tenderness and care, the old man helps you adjust yourself to a seated position and begins to gently pick woodchip flakes out of your hair.

"What are you?" you ask in fear as you gaze at the stranger. He says nothing.

"That ringing in my head, was that you?" There is still no response. "Answer me!" you yell, leaning back out of the old man's reach.

"I am called Emmanuel," the stranger says affectionately. "I have been tasked to watch over you. He who sent me has buried gifts inside of you. He now wishes for a return on his investment."

Your mind is riddled with questions, and they all come out at once. "Who sent you? What gifts do I possess? Why now?"

With a smile, the old man stares into the distance before aiming his piercing gaze at yours and speaking. "How long will you continue to flee from yourself? Is it not apparent that you have been selected?"

"Selected for what?" you ask, beginning to grow wary of Emmanuel's mysterious words. You watch as the smile on his face stretches even wider.

"May I show you?" he asks. In fear of another dose of the knocking, and eager for any clarification, you hesitantly nod yes. You watch as Emmanuel slowly reaches out his arm and touches two of his bony fingers to your forehead. You begin to feel queasy, and your vision starts to blur. "Relax child," he utters softly as images begin to flash before your eyes. "All is well."

***

You are in a dreamlike state. You cannot see your hands or feel any of your other extremities. There is no noise. You have no body, just a consciousness: a cerebral awareness of the strange new world around you.

"Where am I?" you wonder to yourself as you float through the darkness. A few seconds ago, you were sitting in the woodchips with the old man, and now there is no sight of him—or of anything for that matter, just a void of blackness engulfing every direction. A tiny flicker of light begins to shine in the distance, like a pinhole made in the roof of a tent. As you drift closer to the light, it grows in size, and its rays gradually become more intense. Before you know it, your surroundings have shifted. Brightness has overtaken you, and for a brief moment, you can see nothing but white. Gradually, the intensity of the light fades away, and you find yourself walking through a hallway you do not recognize.

Thankful to once again possess legs to walk with, while simultaneously feeling the fear associated with this bizarre experience, you slowly creep down the hallway toward a door that has been left ajar. Anticipation mounts with every step as you approach it. You somehow know that your entire life has been building up to this reveal. You can feel it in your subconscious: "My destiny is behind this door." As you draw nearer, you can hear two muffled voices speaking softly to each other. The closer you move, the more distinct the voices become. With your heart pounding harder than you thought humanly possible, you gently press your palm against the white door and carefully ease it forward, creating a space big enough to fit your head through. As daintily as a mouse, you poke your head into the opening and gaze upon what is inside. There are two people wrapped in a lover's embrace. They are lying on a bed watching television.

One of them is a woman. She is the most beautiful creature you have ever laid eyes upon. You are transfixed by her. Your eyes can do nothing but soak in the splendor of her smile and every curve of her body. She is magnificent. You have never seen the woman before, but there is an overwhelming sensation that you know her. Something about her is familiar, and you feel connected to her.

"Having fun?" Emmanuel whispers from behind you. Startled, you leap backward, crouching to avoid being seen by the couple. "They cannot see you," Emmanuel says and laughs reassuringly. "This is all for you."

"Who was that woman?" you ask, trying to calm yourself down. "I feel like I've seen her before."

Emmanuel's eyes light up with a smile as he leans all of his weight on his cane. "I think you are asking the wrong question. I believe you should be asking, who is that man?"

You are not sure how much more of this your heart can take, but as it begins to accelerate yet again, you recognize that in the brief time you peeked into the room, you had not bothered to look at the man the woman was lying next to. Standing up, you cautiously approach the door once more, push it forward, and take a gander. The shock knocks you to your knees. Your arms become weak, and you stare speechless into the couple's bedroom, unable to move a muscle. The man is tall, about six foot two, with broad shoulders and curly hair. He is lying beneath the woman as she rests on his chest. Their hands are interlocked. You watch as the woman lovingly kisses the man's knuckles while he channel surfs with the remote in his opposite hand.

"He's . . . me," you gasp as tears begin to well up in your eyes. The man shares all of your facial features. He looks to be in his early thirties, and the peach fuzz that collects unevenly under your chin appears to have grown into a dark, well-manicured beard on his face.

"We finally did it," he says, rubbing his palm across the woman's belly.

"You're going to be such a good father," she whispers tenderly. The two of them stare into each other's eyes before leaning in for a passionate kiss. Then everything goes black.

***

Your eyes open, and you are back at the park, sitting next to Emmanuel in the woodchips. "More, let me see more!" you yell frantically, grasping Emmanuel's cloak. "Please," you beg, ignoring the lump in your throat. "I must see more."

"You have seen enough, my child," Emmanuel says sternly.

"Is that . . . my wife?" you ask timidly.

"She's waiting for you," Emmanuel says happily. "She's waiting for you to grow up."

"She said I was going to be a great father." You stare at Emmanuel with disbelieving eyes. "But I don't even want kids."

"You do." Emmanuel nods in confirmation of the fact. "You just never thought there was anyone out there who would love you."

"There isn't!" you snap back defensively as tears begin to fall. "Everyone has left me. I have no one. Derrick stabbed me in the back, I have nothing in common with Jared, I barely talk to my dad, I've broken Kendra . . . I'm a monster."

Your face is drenched now, but you don't care. You've been holding this in for twenty-one years now. Everything is coming out.

"You underestimate the work that has been done to prosper you," says Emmanuel as he swipes his thumb across your cheek, wiping away your tears. "I was not sent here as a spy. I was sent as a guide."

"What kind of guide would let me hurt so many people?" you ask angrily. "What kind of guide leaves me alone for so long?"

Emmanuel plunges his cane deep into the ground. With nearly all of his fleeting strength, he uses the staff to push himself upward to a standing position. Groaning as his bones settle, the old man gazes down upon you. "Gifts do not always come wrapped the way you expect them to, Myles. Do you not take for granted the teachings of Ethan? And what of your brother Joshua?"

You imagine the look on Ethan's face when he heard how drastically your numbers had increased since he last departed. You are so tired of letting him down. You are tired of wasting his time.

You remember Ethan urging you to put away this lifestyle and be a good example to your younger brother, Joshua. Joshua is your eighteen-year-old brother. He did not grow up quiet like you did; in fact, he is just the opposite of you. He has naturally possessed the characteristics you struggled your entire life to obtain. In high school, Joshua was the life of the party that you were never invited to. As you grew into young men, you shared a similar recklessness with women and fun that leaves you empty inside. Though unbeknownst to most people, and hidden beneath his larger-than-life persona, Joshua is a compassionate human being with a good heart but a lack of direction. The two of you hadn't been close until the day he caught you in the bathroom writing your suicide note. A handful of pills had been grouped together nearby on the counter. You had decided that there was no point to life and had desired an end to the constant conflict between your feelings and reality.

Joshua had confronted you about the pills, leading you to break down and finally let someone in. You talked to each other for hours that night, bulldozing the years of walls built between the two of you. The conversation had ended with you wrapping each other in a tearful embrace, thus solidifying your lifelong brotherly bond to have each other's backs regardless of the circumstances. Ethan and Joshua have always been there to wipe the dirt from your eyes and urge you to get back up again. You don't know where you would be without them. Emmanuel was right; you do take them for granted.

"I know there are only two people, my child, but—"

"They are the only two I need," you utter quietly.

"For the moment," Emmanuel says warmly.

You want to hear the old man out, but your mind steers you away from peace. "But why me?" you ask, unable to accept that your life may have a purpose after all. "Why go through all this trouble to help someone like me?"

"Why not you?" asks Emmanuel suspiciously.

"I've hurt a lot of people," you say, shaking your head. "Katie will never get her virginity back, Kendra will never forgive me, and I'll probably never see Marcy again. That vision you showed me can't be true. I can't find a wife. I've been a monster since the third grade. This is who I am."

Emmanuel stares at you in disbelief. "We both know that is not true. I am the tingle in your spine that has followed you throughout your life, pleading with you to step out of your past. I am the nagging in the back of your mind that has urged you not to invest too much of yourself in Jared or Derrick. I let you be in the crowd but not of it."

Emmanuel extends one of his brittle arms down to where you are sitting. "Take my hand," he says with empathy shining in his red eyes. "Let me help you."

A new batch of tears is brewing in your eyes as you fight to hold them back. How can this man know all the pain you have caused and still want to help you? You had even spit in his face the first time you met.

You stare at the old man's wrinkly hand. "I am not a good person," you finally say, looking down.

Unable to meet Emmanuel's eyes, you listen as he calmly says the words that bring you to tears once again. "I don't recall asking if you were one."

You begin to sob uncontrollably as you come to the realization that there is a way out of this cycle of misery you have been stuck in. You glance up at Emmanuel, who is smiling harder than ever, his hand still extended to you. "You can take my hand now, Myles, and we will move along on this journey through life together. Or you can continue to spend your days at the mercy of the little things. The choice is up to you."

After a few moments of hesitation, and over twenty-one years' worth of weeping, you confidently grasp Emmanuel's hand in yours. Then you stand up and wrap your arms around his feeble body. As his fragile fingers rest upon your back, you sob tears of joy and hope onto his soft white robe. You feel like fighting again. You feel a sense of contentment far greater than even Jane had been able to provide. You bury your head in his shoulder and thank him for watching over you. You thank him for Ethan and Joshua, and all the second chances you have received throughout the years. For the first time in your life, you know that everything is going to be all right.

Michael Wade

About the Author

Michael Wade is an Instructional Assistant and college student at Cal State Dominguez Hills. He enjoys writing, film, comics, and weight training. Michael writes short stories, screenplays, music, and poetry. He looks forward to publishing more books in the future.

Enjoy the following poem. This is a sample of what will be coming in the future.

Black Sheep
by Michael Wade

You stalked me like a Wolfpack, felt your presence but pulled back. The change in me was obvious; you know I never could act.

I ignored the warnings. In school, I had poor performance.

I admit my mind and soul was weak, sowing seeds, skipping poetry. Feeling something's off, but deep down I know it's me. Hopefully, this broken piece of a hole that's me can know the peace that I won't achieve if I don't believe. I was a pessimistic, sex addicted, depressed and rigid, less than timid kid who was blessed and gifted.

You helped me get my head right. I was born to spread light. Momma was my fairy, hated to say bye Sherri. Going to school without her was quite scary. Sat alone in the corner of the library.

She had all the answers face it, never thought she'd be a cancer patient, faith was her only chance to make it so she beat it that's amazin.

I didn't know what this force was that protected her, now I know that it loved me, I don't possess the words, to say thanks, so I brushed it off like a dusty cloth when you've played pranks. I'm flying on golden wings this heart was of broken dreams. One man stands in my way...only me. So this is my thank you letter. Pain only makes me better. Bathe in your grace forever. It's an honor to serve you; it's my grateful pleasure.